Flames

Without

By Joseph J. R. Johnson

For my parents.
Thanks for all the support,
Through all the years.

Prologue

Lightning danced amongst the angry, purple clouds. The frantic jig taking the electric dancers from thunderhead to thunderhead, leaping and flashing in the dark sky. Quick as a snake, one would touch down upon the brows of the mountains, cause a crash and a ruckus then return to tango above. The booming drums of thunder followed the chaotic dance in the murky depths of storm brewed skies. Then, with a culminating ensemble of heavenly drums and blinding white flashes, the lightning dancers came together as one, diving like an eagle into the dry mountain valley. An old tree exploded. Its wooden bones sheared from its body by the energy of the heavenly dancers. The trees and bushes and tall brown grasses gasped at the sight, and the fear, as the valley was lit by the fire the dancers brought. The water in the bushes' branches hissed in dismay as the heat enshrouded the forest. The trees' applause came from the cracking of branches, the popping of pine needles, the crash of falling limbs. The dancing imps of fire cavorted through the valley, painting all in the colors of flame and smoke. Thus, the mountains burned.

*****

Day One: The Man Covered in Ash

Over the rise stumbled the stranger covered in ash. He leaned against a tree for rest, peering down at the valley below him, worried but glad to have nearly reached his destination. Below him, stretching through the valley, lay the city Bergamot. The stranger looked up at the barren mountain peak at the head of the valley. Barely visible stood the watch tower. The tower's beacon sprung alight. With a sigh and a deluge of grey ash, the stranger pushed away from the tree. He had been spotted by the watchers in the tower, their telescopes were as far seeing as ever.

The stranger dove back into the trees, following an old path carved into the side of the steep valley. The pine trees hid him from sight, but he knew soldiers were on their way to pick him up now. He wanted to turn and run back out of the valley. He wished to leave these treacherous mountains, but first he must warn the other cities, though they may be enemies. Below, the sounds of a fast running creek could be heard. The stranger smiled and willed his aching bones to move quicker. He hoped to wash the ash off before coming before Bergamot's council.

Luck was not his. Waiting for him around the last bend in the trail before reaching the creek was a group of five Bergamot soldiers. Two with swords drawn, three with bows pulled taut. The stranger laid out his hands, palms up and empty, in front of himself, and smiled at the sight of the black mud and creeping moss around the flowing waters.

*****

<u>180 Hours Remain</u>

The council chambers lay quiet and peaceful in the tired midday sun. The old councilors sat about the open aired circle of stones. To an outsider the old men and women would appear to be in heavy discussions about policy and philosophy in their small groups, but the approaching soldier knew the councilors were more than likely only gossiping and complaining.

The soldier stopped just outside the ring of standing stones with his ash covered prisoner and waited to be called in. He could not bring himself to blame the councilors for their laziness. One of the first Dynasts of Bergamot had designated the ancient ring of standing stones to be the council chambers of Bergamot and forbade council business to be done elsewhere. He claimed that being outside while discussing the future of Bergamot would help remind the councilors of what is important. Small wildflowers poked colorful heads out from the base of stones. A chipmunk scurried over a broken pillar. Below the council chambers, stretched the city of Bergamot, and behind the chambers rose the Dynast's palace. From the council's vantage could be seen all they should protect, the village, the life of the mountains, and the royal family and military. The true trick of this plan, however, was seen during early spring, late fall, and winter, when the weather was turbulent and violent. The councilors did their business in the snow, and the rain. They huddled amongst the old stones speaking of city policy and wishing to return to the warmth of their own hearths. In the colder months, council business was performed quickly and efficiently, the councilors only discussing the most important issues and quickly coming to decisions. In the warm months, however, the weather in Bergamot was pleasant and mild. The councilors would laze about the stones and little actual business was performed.

Inside the stones the councilors saw the soldier and his prisoner. The quiet conversations died down and the political leader formed a circle in the center of the stone ring. They beckoned the soldier to enter.

Once inside, Servat, one of the senior councilors, asked, "Scion, why do you bring this man here? Judgement of crimes is under the jurisdiction of your grandfather the Dynast."

Scion replied, "Dynast Epath, my grandfather, is being sent the prisoner's message. I deemed his message more relevant to the council and decided that you should hear what he has to say yourselves. If what he says is true, then we must act quickly. Now, soldier of Mica, speak."

The prisoner spoke, "I am from the city of Mica."

Servat and a few of the other councilors snorted in derision.

One councilor said, "We know you hail from our old enemy. Did we not lose fifty men just last year fighting off your goat thieves, and saboteurs?"

The prisoner covered in ash continued, "We are enemies no more. Mica is gone."

Silence save for the buzzing of bees filled the council chambers. The elderly councilors waited to hear more.

"Mica is destroyed," said the man covered in ash. "It burned. We drew too much water into our irrigation canals from the streams and rivers. Our lands were overladen with fruit and vegetables, but the valleys and slopes around us were dry and near barren. The gods sent lightning down from the heavens and fire raced through the valleys whose waters we stole."

Servat interrupted the prisoner, saying, "Yes, yes, and the fire burned your city. What does this have to do with us? The mountain above us provides us with our water. It collects the rain and the snow, fills our two lakes and winding stream, and makes the valley air humid and filled with the smell of wildflowers. A fire cannot touch us here."

The prisoner replied, "You have not laid eyes upon this fire. It has the hunger of a bear in early spring, and the power of a midwinter avalanche. Your valley, though it is wetter than my old home's, will burn all the same."

The councilors muttered amongst themselves. Servat gestured for Scion to take the prisoner and leave.

*****

174 Hours Remain

The court having closed for the day, the Dynast of Bergamot, Epath, sat back in his throne. The old man sighed and reached for his drinking horn. He frowned down at the clear water in the horn then opened his mouth to order a servant to fetch a horn of wine. Before he could order anything, however, the door to the throne room opened and Epath's grandson, Scion, entered.

The Dynast quickly took a swig of water and asked, "Scion, to what do I owe the pleasure? Hopefully, you haven't come for business. The court is closed. I've done all the leading and ruling I needed to today."

Scion frowned at the old, gray haired king, saying, "Are you so worried about being overworked in your old age? Do not worry, I am not here strictly for business. I brought a prisoner to the city jail today."

Epath raised his hand to stop Scion. "This sounds like business. Before you continue," he said while waving at a nearby servant, "I need a drink. Some wine would be excellent."

The servant bowed and quickly left to get his lord a drink.

"Now continue," the Dynast ordered.

Scion continued, "I brought in a prisoner today from Mica. I was wondering if the council had told you anything."

Epath shook his head. He said, "No news about Mica today. Was the prisoner a messenger for war? It's about time they wanted to fight again. It's been almost ten years since the last real war with them. Well in any case, I will hear the news tomorrow and give his sentence then. I'm tired."

The Dynast began standing up.

"You're always tired, grandfather," stated Scion. The less well-trained servants in the throne room gasped, all eyes were on Epath to see his reaction. Scion quickly continued speaking, "The prisoner did not come here for war. He warns of a fire, my lord. He claims it is coming and will destroy us. We should be preparing ourselves."

Epath sat back down, his girth causing the throne to groan under him. The king scowled at his grandson and said, "That was improper. I dismissed the topic of discussion for later, and you continued the topic. The court is closed for the day, I have not been brought this news by the council, and this news comes from a citizen of Mica. First, do you trust this messenger? He could be a spy, a saboteur from Mica, here to spread fear throughout our city. Secondly, if there is a fire, what to do about that fire lies mostly in the hands of the council. I judge the people's disputes, lead our military, and oversee the treasury. The council does..." the Dynast waved his hand distractedly, "Other government minutia. They will come to me when they have discussed and come up with a plan of action, and if it is a good plan, I will fund it. Now, court is over."

Scion bowed and turned to leave.

"Actually, Scion, would you like to join me for dinner? I've seen less of you since you joined the Watch."

The young soldier turned and replied, "Of course I'll join you, grandfather. The palace food is the best in the city."

*****

A Future Day: The Runner
No Time Remains for Him

The message runner crested the ridge, wheezing in the smoky air. He fell to his knees. Bergamot was close. The cobbled road wound through one more valley, up another ridge, along the ridge's long crest, then down and up again, and there would be mild Bergamot, bursting with color and bubbling with water.

He would not reach Bergamot.

The day after Scion had had dinner with his grandfather, the Dynast, the council still had not reported the fire to the king. Scion, taking matters into his own hands, had sent a runner along the road to Mica, to see the fire and report back.

The runner knew he would not reach Bergamot.

The runners of Bergamot were fast. They trained by racing up Mount Van. Whoever was fastest at the noon race was awarded goat meat for dinner. Whoever lapped the mountain course the most from sunrise to sunset was awarded a horn of the finest wine from the Dynast's stores. This runner had never achieved either, but he was far from being the slowest. He had run from Bergamot on the morning of the second day after the arrival of the man covered in ash and had run for five days. He had run under darkening skies, thickening air, and finally smoke.

The runner looked back. He had trouble breathing. Smoke clogged his breath, stung his eyes, coated his nose in its acrid stench. He quickly looked forward, willfully forgetting what he had seen behind him.

He could not return home.

The road turned below him as it entered the valley. It ran roughly parallel to what the man wanted to run directly away from. The fire would catch him in the valley. He closed his eyes, then opened them again. He would rather see the smoke-filled valley below, than the terror of fire that appeared behind his closed lids.

The runner knew he could not return home.

He stood unsteadily. Running without break for a day, a night, and another day from the fire had tired his muscles, the ash and smoke had weakened his lungs, fear had taken his mind. He stumbled down the slope to the valley floor. The runner was quicker than the fire. He had gained ground on the fire, but not nearly enough. Willing his legs to move he continued doggedly down the winding road, taking a little comfort from the small stream running next to him. Soon ash would turn the clear, cool waters to blackened sludge.

The runner knew that if he did not return home, there might not be a home to return to.

The runner stumbled and fell. He hissed as the stones broke open the skin on his knees. Then he heard something that made him shiver. The silent valley, already devoid of animals and insects in the face of the coming fire, quietened further. The air stood still. Only the stream made noise and that seemed muted in the stillness of the moment. Far above, a golden lining appeared upon the ridge. The valley air rushed upwards to feed the flames. Ash billowed down. The grey sky turned black, the world burned orange. Rivulets of tears streaked the runner's ash covered face as the burning harbingers of hell swept down towards the valley floor.

The runner never returned home.

*****

Day Three: Barrel Hoarding
131 Hours Remain

News of the fire spread through Bergamot the day after Scion's runner left. The city was buzzing with worry. The Dynast Epath's throne room filled with concerned citizens. Scion watched from the side of the room. He had taken the day off from the Watch to see if the council would broach the topic of the fire, and if they did not then Scion himself would bring it to the court's attention.

The Dynast lazily waved his hand for the next petitioner.

The court scribe called out, "Mathilda of the Lower Lake District!"

Mathilda, a middle-aged woman from the richest district in the city, stepped forward. She bowed quickly to the Dynast and began her petition. "My Lord, I cannot buy any barrels, baskets, pots, or buckets."

Epath stared down at her for a few seconds.

Mathilda twitched nervously under the ruler's seemingly disinterested gaze. She broke the silence, saying, "I need something to hold water in. If I don't have something to hold water, then I won't be able to wet my house's roof when the fire comes. People have apparently been buying out the coopers', and potters', and weavers' wares so that they can have all the water they need for this fire." The distraught woman turned to the rest of the throne room and continued, "What about the rest of us? We need water! Are you fine with letting your neighbor's house burn down as long as you are safe under your properly and probably overwetted thatch? We all need a barrel to hold water. We need to all be ready, and we all have to have the tools to be ready. Don't selfishly hoard your barrels, and if I see any of you trying to resell barrels at higher prices, I may just start a new fire in your homes! See how your excess barrels like that."

Epath struck the ground with his spear and said in the quickly quieting court, "What are these rumors of fire?"

Servat stepped forward from the back of the throne room and answered, "Your majesty, a messenger from Mica came to us two days ago with warnings of a wildfire that destroyed his city."

The scribe called out, "The throne recognizes Councilman Servat."

The Dynast snorted. "Ah yes, I was told of this fire. And good riddance to the Micans. They were always such a violent clan. So, what of this fire? Has the truth of the messenger's words been asserted?"

"No, Dynast, sir," Servat answered. "We have not seen the fire ourselves. The council believes this may be a trap by Mica. We believe that this may be a ruse to scare us into using up resources to fend off a fire, and while we are busy preparing for fire they will attack. They may even be hoping we will abandon the city in fear, leaving it open for them to take without a fight."

Epath raised his hand and said, "But they cannot think we are so brainless as to prepare for fire from just one man's warning. And we would never abandon the city until all hope is lost."

Servat nodded in agreement. "I agree with you, my lord," the councilman said. "But what if they start a fire the next mountain over? To the Watch it would appear as if the messenger's fire were true. And for the city folk, the ash and smoke from the nearby fire mixed with the warnings from the messenger could cause panic. This is what we fear they are planning."

Epath sat back in thought. He said, "If that is Mica's plan then that is a surprisingly tricky plan for berry pickers, and wheat farmers. I like it. Maybe in a few years we can do something similar. However, right now, we do not know one way or the other if this is a wildfire or a Mican trick. Wildfire is not a military matter. I leave the preparations for that to the council. I will not open the treasury to the council for fire related projects until the fire is known and apparent, in case this truly is a military ploy by the Micans."

"What of the barrel hoarding?" Mathilda asked.

The Dyanst looked down at the middle-aged women and stated, "More barrels will be made. If you want the coopers to work faster, you will have to complain to them yourself."

"My lord," Scion called out as he stepped forward into the center of the throne room.

The scribe announced, "The throne recognizes Scion son of Char son of Epath."

Scion bowed to his grandfather, straightened himself, and said, "My lord, I have an idea that would protect against both fire and war. My idea is to dig a large trench at the head of the valley and fill the trench with water. If the fire comes, the fire will not be able to cross a wide trench, thus saving the city, as long as the trench is wide enough. If an army comes, they will have a difficult time crossing such a trench while we bombard them with arrows. If we fill this trench with water to make a moat, it would be even more effective against both threats. Would you fund this project? In either case, war or fire, a moat would benefit us."

Epath stroked his beard thoughtfully, then said, "A good idea, Scion. I will provide money for tools and send some palace servants to help. You will be in charge of this project; however, you are not excused from your work on the Watch. I will discuss your workload with your commander. Begin building tomorrow. I feel time is of the essence in this matter, whether it be fire or war that comes hungrily to our door."

Scion bowed and returned to his spot at the side of the room.

*****

<u>120 Hours Remain</u>

That night the sun bled crimson into the serrated mountain horizon as it set behind a wall of smoke in the distance. Scion watched apprehensively. Never had a sunset looked so menacing. This was proof of the fire in the distance, but the sight was fleeting and only seen by the Watch in their sturdy tower atop the mountain peak. Scion knew Servat and his grandfather would be dubious of the warnings provided from a too red sunset.

*****

Day Four: The Beginning of a Solution
112 Hours Remain

"I think we should build the moat along here," said councilwoman Pulful, pointing to the curve in the valley that marked the separation point between the Costilleja District and the Harebell District. "This area is the thinnest section of the valley and would be the easiest to build a wide trench across."

Scion frowned, saying, "That would be the easiest place to build, but what of the Costilleja District? They will be left to fend for themselves. We will have to come up with an evacuation plan and make provisions for them when they become refugees. We will have to rebuild the district."

Rustling of grass gave warning of someone's approach. Scion, Pulful, and the palace servants assigned to help Scion turned to look for the newcomer. Servat slowly wound his way around the standing stones of the Council Chambers and came to stand next to his fellow councilwoman.

"How goes ditch digging?" Servat asked. "Surely you won't build the trench all the way up here? We are above tree line, at the edge of a large cliff. Fire cannot reach here, and even if it did, there is nothing but short grass and stunted bushes for tinder. The fire would die." Servat looked about himself as if to make sure his assertions of what grew on the peak were correct. Then he continued, "Also, is there some kind of festival today? I've smelled a bonfire all morning but can't figure out where or why it is burning."

Scion replied, "We are deciding where to build the trench. I think we should construct it at the edge of the city. Pulful says we should build it between Costilleja and Harebell. What do you think, Servat?"

Servat pondered the map of the city for some time then answered, "I agree with Pulful, which is rare I might add." Pulful chuckled in appreciation of the joke. "That area is a thin part of the valley. If speed is the goal, which I assume it is, that would be the best spot."

"What of Costilleja District?" Scion asked.

Servat responded by saying, "What of it? A trench in front of Harebell District will protect Harebell, Lower Lake, and Columbine Palace. It's not like Costilleja would be difficult to make anew. The district is poor and rundown anyway."

Scion scowled. "Those are people's homes! We can't just leave them to the fire."

"Or war," Servat said. "The fire is not yet confirmed."

Scion's scowl deepened, and he clenched his fists.

Pulful quickly spoke up, "I agree, Scion, it would be a tragedy to leave the Costilleja District undefended, but with our timeline, manpower, and budget, what are we to do? Building where you would like would be much riskier for the project's proper finish. And if we don't complete the project fully with a wide enough moat, well then everything will burn. The project would be a waste."

Pulful's reasoned words quieted Scion, who stared at the map, thinking. The councilors silently waited. Scion was heir to the throne, and they dared not disrupt him on his first city project.

Finally, Scion said, "You both make a good point. I understand building at the head of the Harebell District would ensure we make a wide trench in time, but I cannot willfully put one of the city's districts in danger. I will not separate the people of Costilleja from the rest of Bergamot. We build the trench at the head of the valley."

*****

100 Hours Remain

The smell of smoke superseded the usual flowery scent of the blooming city of twilit Bergamot. An old pine-built bar in Harebell District paid host to its usual denizens, and its famous bard.

"Have you seen this?" Asked Marbell as she sat down at a table of friends. She slapped a flyer onto the center of the table for all to see. The flyer stated that the heir apparent, Scion son of Char, was requesting volunteers for a trench building project.

The table leaned forward to read the flyer.

"What are they building a trench for? Is it to hold water when the stream overflows and the valley floods like what happened fifteen years ago?" asked Bystan, a burly sheepherder who worked for Servat.

Marbell quickly replied, "No, it's for the fire. Fire can't leap over deep and wide ditches, or so I hear. This trench was young Scion's idea. I like the lad. I think he'll make a fine Dynast one day, as long as he stays away from his grandfather's wine."

"You're one to talk, Marbell," said the third person at the table, Honis, an honest man who grew and sold herbs outside his hut in the Costilleja District. "In any case, read the flyer out loud. I never learned my letters."

Marbell laughed and took a long swig of her beer, then belched, before replying, "This is beer not wine, so I'm safe from turning into a fat, lazy Dynast. One becomes that way by indulging in the palace wine. Hard earned beer bought from hard earned money, can only make you a better person. They want people. Scion wants volunteers to help dig the ditch."

Honis nodded, saying, "I feel overindulgence in anything can turn you sour, be it wine, beer, or my neighbor's strange plant. Maybe I'll join Scion. If it's to protect the city from fire, then it's a good project. My grandfather spoke of the old fire that burned our valley when he was a child. Apparently, that fire burnt down most of the valley, and the trees didn't recover for thirty years. You can see the old burn scars on the mountain sides. They're the large copses of aspen. And if I help, I might meet Scion and my luck will increase."

"You're a good man, Honis, I wish I could join you," said Marbell. "Apparently there's some outrage about barrel hoarding, and my husband has enough orders to keep him busy till next spring. I'm to help him fill out the orders. Who hoards barrels anyway, for what purpose? Just down the street I saw two people trying to sell used barrels for ridiculous amounts. What about you Bystan?"

Bystan shrugged. "We'll see what Servat says. I'd like to join, but what Servat says goes."

"Ah, poo on the old councilman. We all know he hates poor people. Just ditch work for a few days. Say Scion ordered you." Marbell replied vehemently.

Bystan shrugged, answering, "I wish I could, but if I lose this job, I'll starve this winter. I haven't earned enough for all the grain I need. I hear in the lowlands the summers last longer and the winters are milder. I hear that someone on my wages would be able to work longer into the fall, and thus earn more money."

Honis smiled good naturedly as he exasperated, "You always speak of the lowlands with longing. It's so much better in the lowlands, you claim. Long summers, mild winters, wheat fields stretching from horizon to horizon, who could even believe that? There isn't that much flat land anywhere. Look, Bystan, you live here, and sure Bergamot may be bad sometimes, but it is no better anywhere else. Here we're protected by steep valley sides, and a good military. The mountain ensures consistent rain and snowmelt every year, even when the surrounding lands are struck by drought. I hear the lowlands suffer from scorching summers, and violent thunderstorms. I've even heard of strange spirits called tornados that sweep the lands and tear up entire cities. You're better off here. And we'd be sad if you left."

"I know, I know," said Bystan. "I could not leave anyway. I don't have the funds. But I do have the funds for the next round."

Marbell and Honis cheered their approval of another round of drinks as Bystan went to the bar.

*****

96 Hours Remain

That night smoke crept up the valley and settled in bed with Bergamot. A few asthmatic children, who already lived tough lives in the high mountain valley's thin air, died in their sleep. Smoke strangled their throats in the dark. Their deaths were determined by the local healers and priests to be related to their asthma and the pollen from the pine trees and wildflowers. Fire, they claimed, kills through burning, not suffocating.

*****

Day Five: Indecision and Misinformation
87 Hours Remain

Early morning mist filled Juniper Valley. The normally sparkling fog was dull white under the grey skies. Bystan let his eyes wander from Servat's goats. They would be fine. Bystan had trained them well, and when he called, he knew they would return. He sighed despondently. He was not sure if the grey sky was from the fire or just strange low-lying clouds. Many in the city, including Servat, claimed the sky was not that abnormal. They stated days like this came often to their valley. Bystan wondered about that. He had never seen clouds that covered the whole world in such uniform haze. These were not pearly white snow clouds, or black thunderheads, these clouds, or whatever they were, were something else. The haze made Bystan uneasy, and he was not alone in this regard. The goats were also jumpy this morning. Bystan did not blame them. The weird light made it difficult to see properly. Everything was flat, without shadow, or definition. The usual piney smell of Juniper Valley was covered by the smell of smoke. Many people, Servat included, claimed the smoke smell was from nearby Micans burning bonfires to scare the Bergamotians, since they were the ones who started the rumors of wildfire.

Bystan sighed and rubbed his head. The haze and smoke smell made him think of forest fire, but people smarter and richer than he claimed the wildfire was a hoax created by Bergamot's ancient enemy, Mica. But then again, Scion, heir to the throne seemed to think the fire was real, wasn't that what Marbell claimed was the purpose of the trench? But then this morning Bystan had heard that the Dynast was only funding Scion's project because it would provide another means of defense if Mica attacked Bergamot. Therefore, the trench building was not about the fire at all, but about war.

The trench project. Bystan wanted to help. Whether the trench was for war or fire, he wanted to help. Standing by and watching while rumors of destruction swirled about made him uneasy. Everyone else seemed to be doing something about the war or fire, whichever they believed to be the truth, while Bystan simply tended to Servat's goats like every other day.

Bystan had asked Servat if he and some of the other employees of Servat could help dig the trench. Servat had replied, "You may if you wish. It is volunteer work. Scion will not pay you, and I will not pay you either while you are away. You must also remember, any losses to my income due to your absence will be felt by all of us. Say you work at the trench for a week. I will have to find an interim goatherd, one who probably is not nearly as good as you, Bystan. After all you are a very skilled and valuable goatherd. This interim herder will not tend to my goats properly. This may lead to my goats not eating properly this week. The milk product for this week will therefore be less than usual. It may be so bad as to force me to let go of some employees. I do run a tight estate after all. What if this interim goatherd loses or accidentally kills a goat. What then? A single good goat is worth more than what most of my servants make in a year. It is a risk, but since the trench is an altruistic project, I will allow you to help Scion if you wish, but be warned the risk does not lie just to my estate, but also to all of my employees. We must all work together to keep this enterprise running."

So, Bystan had stayed and tended to the goats, but felt no better for the decision. Below him the valley rolled away over juniper bushes and lichen ladened boulders. This valley, which ran nearly parallel to Bergamot's valley, was accessed by an animal trail running over the ridge that separated the two valleys. Bystan enjoyed the quiet valley, with its smell of pine, warm air, and unobstructed sky. Many said the valley was Mount Van's forgotten child due to the rain collected by the mountain's soaring head being sent down to Bergamot and almost never to Juniper Valley.

"I feel like I'm forgotten too, Juniper," Bystan said, addressing the valley. "Most everyone I know either has a family or business to run. I have none of that. They know how to read and add. I get my news from hearsay and trust I am not swindled. The world moves and I am slow to catch up. Slow to get news, slow to act."

Out from behind a juniper bush below wandered a fox family. They looked haggard. The family stared up at Bystan, then fell on their sides. The luxurious coat of the animals was splotched, gray with ash. Bystan quickly stood up. Foxes were not a problem for goats but judging by the foxes' fur and their lack of fear, Bystan figured that the fox family must have run from the nearby fire. If foxes were forced from their burrows, other animals would be coming soon as well. Bystan called for the goats.

The goats came one after another. They jumped and hopped out from the bushes and bleated their greetings to their keeper. Bystan noted that many of the goats walked right past the foxes, sensing no danger from the refugees. This reinforced Bystan's concerns about the fire. If animals were fleeing the flames, then soon a bear or bobcat or lion would appear in the valley, and they would love nothing more than to eat goat or Bystan. It was time to leave. The goats had eaten enough juniper for the day.

*****

82 Hours Remain

The trench was well underway if, according to Pulful, you wanted to build a long, shallow divot for tripping people in the mud instead of a moat. Two hundred volunteers slowly dug out the ditch while trading gossip. Scion watched unhappily.

"Why the sour face, my lord?" Asked Pulful. The middle-aged councilwoman was taking a break from digging to get a drink of water.

"The work goes slowly. We need to work faster if we are to beat the fire," answered Scion.

Pulful took a long look at the volunteers while she drank her cool water. She replied, "True, they are slow. But they are volunteers. They take this as an opportunity to help the community and an excuse to do something different with their day. If you make this a job for them, they will leave, even if the fire burns just down the valley from here. You've been trained in the military your whole life, correct?"

Scion nodded.

Pulful continued, "Then you are used to hard work and being told what to do. You are used to being led by heavy hands. This sort of project needs to be led with soft hands. If you want them to work faster, give them an incentive."

"Like what?"

Pulful shrugged, while saying, "I am not sure. I would ask them if I were you."

Scion grunted, grabbed his shovel, and went down into the narrow ditch. He positioned himself in the center of the work and began digging as quickly as he could. He hoped the others near him would see how much harder he was working and try to keep up. Instead the person next to Scion stood up with a sigh and leaned on his pickaxe. Scion was about to stop and yell at the man when the man broke the silence first.

"Marbell! Did you decide to join us and dig a hole? It's great fun!" The man said, not entirely sincerely.

The woman passing by answered, "No, Honis, I'm coming to collect the barrels my husband and I loaned to Pulful for holding water for the workers. Can you believe there's a line out our door for barrels? Coopers are supposed to work hard before harvest so that people can store that which they sow and to keep beer for the winter, not work night and day during the middle of the summer. This is ridiculous. There was even a fist fight when one customer was seen buying two barrels. We need all the barrels we can get."

Scion looked up and saw a soot covered woman in a leather apron. The woman looked over at Scion and her eyes went wide and she quickly tried dusting off her apron, which did little good.

Scion held up his hand and said, "No need to fuss, lady. It is not like we are any cleaner. Thank you for the water barrels."

Honis looked from Marbell to Scion and asked, "You know each other?"

Marbell stared blankly at Honis for a few seconds then started laughing. She wheezed out, "You said... You said that maybe you'd meet Lord Scion... and, and... hahaha, your luck would improve. And then... you work right next to him and do not even know. You fool, Honis!"

Honis looked around at the workers trying to ascertain who could be the prince. Scion watched in mild confusion. He had only ever been in the palace or the military where he was treated no differently than anyone else. Honis looked back at Marbell questioningly, and Marbell jerked her head towards Scion. Honis visibly jumped away from Scion, then bent to one knee.

Honis said, "It is an honor to help you make this great trench, my lord. I hope it will keep the fire at bay."

Scion blushed a deep red and replied, "Well, thank you, but I should be thanking you. You volunteered. You left your businesses to help me. Are you not losing money? Actually, I was wondering, what would be a reasonable reward for this work? Tell me, what would you want from me in exchange for your help?"

Honis looked up, dumbfounded. He said, "Oh do not worry sir. All of my herbs were bought out today. Barrels are not the only thing worth hoarding for a fire. It seems basil is very desirable as a fire deterrent as well. As for a reward, sir, I think just this conversation may be enough."

Scion frowned. Maybe this is why his grandfather never left the palace.

Scion said, "Do not lie, Honis, I am a poor conversationalist, and even if I wasn't, I doubt that speaking to me would be much reward for anything. What are you going to do when you leave here today? What do you think most people will do?"

"I'm going to the tavern after I pick up these barrels," said Marbell. "Assuming my husband lets me. There are so many orders."

Scion laughed and said, "That's a good answer. So, Honis, beer or wine, which do you prefer?"

Honis immediately replied, "Beer, sir, and if possible, could you get a barrel that isn't watered down? Your grandfather waters the beer. He claims it's to stop bar fights, but really it's to make the beer last longer, and make a good profit." Honis turned bright red as he realized that he had just insulted the Dynast in front of the Dynast's grandson.

Scion replied happily, "Beer it is then! I'll be sure to get thick, dark beer for you. Then, when we all drink our fill tonight, I will send the barrels over to your place, Marbell."

Marbell thanked the prince and collected her barrels. Word spread down the line of diggers about the boon of beer, and as morale improved, the work went quicker. By the end of the day the trench was as deep as half a man, but woefully thin. Scion worried about the speed of digging. Pulful was pleasantly surprised at how efficiently Scion had rallied the people.

That night a bonfire was lit next to the trench and the volunteers had their fill of beer and bread. The young volunteers, full of the vast stamina of youth, spent the evening dancing amongst the wildflowers and under the pine boughs. The older workers sat around in a circle trading stories of Bergamot's past. Scion listened intently. These were stories he had never heard while in the palace or the watchtower. He had only ever heard fairytales or war stories there. Those stories always ended with morals or the glory of Bergamot. The stories told on that smoky evening were stories without purpose. Stories filled with love, mirth, and nostalgia. Stories without true endings, for the characters were still there, still around in Bergamot. The volunteers spun old feuds and mistakes into mirthful tales of village life. Scion could not get enough. His tutors would say that the stories told that night had no literary purpose and should be forgotten, but Scion fell in love with them anyway, and would remember them fondly.

*****

<u>72 Hours Remain</u>

That night the streets of the Costilleja district played host to a vast herd of deer. The tired animals stopped their desperate flight from fire to rest in the peaceful, cool valley filled with the sounds and smell of running water. There was peace in the valley, and the animals felt safe. In the early morning, the citizens of Costilleja made a killing off the complacent animals and were provided with enough venison for the rest of the year, provided they too could survive till then.

*****

Day Six: A Protest Against Help
67 Hours Remain

The sun did not rise. It crawled slowly across the hazy heavens as a small red dot, bleeding orange light down to the world. Flowers kept shut their bulbs. Birds did not herald the glory of day. Only the large stream of Bergamot gurgled happily, unconcerned about fire. The volunteers returned to work the trench. They were tired, some hungover. They wheezed and coughed, working through the smoke.

At noon, when the bloodspot sun squelched to heaven's greatest height, priests and businessmen came to watch the trench building. The newcomers stayed quiet when Scion came near, but when the prince left, they extolled their virtues.

"Why are you working for free?" The businessmen asked. "You are freely giving your effort away to the military. This trench will be used as a moat in war. It has nothing to do with helping us, only apathetic Epath and the rich. If you are so desperate to work, then come work for us. We will become rich together. Stop giving away your talents for free."

"Why are you digging a trench?" The priests asked. "The mountain will protect us. It always has. Mount Van collects the rain clouds and drives them down our valley. Mount Van creates a crown of snow that melts into our two lakes and down into our stream. The mountain will fight the fire, not man, for what man can hope to fight against nature. We must pray for rain, not toil uselessly in the dirt. The mountain will hear our pleas and vanquish this fire. Digging a scar into the mountain and diverting the stream will only anger Mount Van, and we will perish for our work."

Scion and Pulful quietly asked the businessmen and priests to leave the dig site. They did so with much grumbling and more proselytizing.

*****

Day Seven: A Riot for Barrels
37 Hours Remain

The streets of Bergamot swarmed like a net filled with fresh caught fish. The heavy orange air and red sun that greeted the citizens of Bergamot that morning had brought fright and anxiety into their lives. The people were worried. They took to the streets and the throngs grew. Many simply did not want to be alone in the weird half-light; they were frightened by the thoughts of fire and war that filled their heads. They needed company to comfort them. Others were filled with the nervous energy of caged animals. They needed to be doing something in order to force their minds to ignore their own anxieties. These two groups filled the streets and instead of finding solace there, they found their insecurities mirrored in all the other faces.

Outside Marbell and her husband's cooper smith, the line of customers was swallowed up by the mass of people. Inside, Marbell dragged a small barrel to the door and peeked out. She gasped as she saw the crowd's silhouette.

"Sweetie," Marbell called into the backroom. "The crowd outside is massive. And have you seen the sunlight? It's red, like the light itself was dipped in blood. Mount Van alone knows what's going on. Could you deliver this barrel? I'll take over the forge for a bit."

The sound of bellows quieted as Marbell's husband, Lac, grunted loudly from the forge. He came out of the backroom and stood next to Marbell. They made an interesting couple. Lac was a full head shorter than Marbell and had the face of a child. Marbell was tall and robust. Both of them had large shoulders and muscular arms from making barrels for a living. Lac peered out, then looked at Marbell with raised eyebrows.

"I know," Marbell said. "You hate dealing with customers. I'm the one who talks a lot and is better suited for taking orders and handing out deliveries. But you saw what it's like out there. It's terrifying. Why are there so many people? Are they all here for barrels? Did Mica attack? Is the fire here already? I don't want to go out there. Please, can you go deliver this?" She asked while holding out the barrel in her hands.

Lac grabbed the barrel, hefted it over his shoulder and grunted, said, "Okay. Wish me luck. Be back in a little."

Lac left. As the door opened the sounds of the crowd filled Marbell's home. She heard the babbling of the people as they milled about. Some people shouted over the crowd adding their own high-strung notes. Marbell caught a few words and phrases through the madness. Snippets of people asking what was happening, what was to be done. People yelling for everyone to stay calm and go about their business as normal. Above it all, in a deep, dismal chant and plea, could be heard the prayers for rain.

Lac disappeared into the crowd. Marbell hoped her husband would find the customer. Their clientele had become angry and impatient. Their demands had kept Marbell and her husband working for the past two nights as they built barrels in place of dreams. Marbell was tired. She shook her head and reminded herself that this was only a passing thing, and anyway they were making incredible profit. Once this all blew over, their hard work would be worth every lost bit of sleep.

The silhouetted crowd moved quicker. As Marbell watched, the amorphous mass of people shifted and convulsed angrily where Lac had disappeared. She gasped and ran to the door, intent on finding her husband. Just as she flung open the entrance, Lac rushed out of the crowd and into the house. He quickly slammed and locked the door. The crowd pressed against the building.

Marbell looked questioningly at Lac.

Lac said, "I delivered to the wrong customer. Second on the waitlist. The correct customer got upset. Might have started a bit of a fight."

The noise seeping through the walls indicated that there was more than a fight happening outside. The people shouted and yelled. The initial catalyst to the unrest, the incorrect delivery and subsequent anger, was quickly forgotten as panic spread through the crowded street. People screamed for something to be done. They demanded the soldiers go out and fight whatever they found outside the valley. They demanded Epath provide shelter and protection from fire. They wanted to know why no one had been taking any of this seriously until now. The mass of people, which had been flowing smooth and laminarly, now turned turbulent.

The people who had until then been yelling for people to go home and calm down were thrown to the ground, as the crowd violently rejected their advice. The people praying for rain were shoved into silence as the mob extolled action over words.

Soldiers pushed down the street to quell the discontent. The mass of citizens bristled at the military. They hurled abuse, saying that the soldiers should be out watching for the fires or teasing out the enemy, not policing the good folk of Bergamot. The soldiers lowered their spears and slowly advanced, pushing the crowd back without harming anyone.

Then Marbell heard from outside, "I just want a barrel! I want a barrel so I can wet my roof when the fire comes. I want to protect my home! Let me protect my family! I want a barrel! Give me a barrel, a basket, anything!"

Lac's eyes widened and he grabbed Marbell. They rushed into the backroom as pounding sounded on their front door. The wooden door shuddered under the blows. Down the street could be heard the muffled yelling and crashes of other buildings being broken into. Lac clung to Marbell eyeing the shaking door nervously. Marbell squeezed Lac tight. The top hinge of the door came loose, causing the door to wobble with each hit from the rioters. Lac broke out of the embrace and ran to pick up his axe. He planted himself in the doorway to the backroom, ready to fight.

Marbell fell back against the wall. The wood behind her thudded as her weight fell upon it. She slammed her fist into the wall, angry, scared tears falling down her cheeks. Suddenly she straightened. She hurried to Lac, turned him towards her and tried to take the axe. Lac resisted with a confused look. Marbell, fearing there was no time to explain, leaned down and kissed Lac, slowly taking the axe from his now relaxed grip. Lac gasped but did not stop Marbell. He trusted her, even in his current panic.

Marbell stepped up to the back wall of their house and swung the axe. The metal bit into the wood. She swung again. Lac, understanding now what she was doing, grabbed a hammer and chisel from the workbench. He knelt underneath Marbell and began chiseling a line in the wall. The thudding from outside came louder and quicker. There was not much time.

"If only," Marbell said in between swings, "We had gotten... a house in Lower Lake. Those houses... have windows."

Lac nodded in fervent agreement.

The axe crunched through the remaining wood of the plank they were working on. Lac stood up and kicked just above his chisel line. The plank fell back leaving behind a jagged line of splinters at knee height. They moved to the next plank. In the front room of the house, the door wobbled and shuddered. The nails holding the lock to the wall inched out with every thundering beat of the rioters' fists. The second plank fell away. Marbell and Lac scurried through the opening into the back alley just as their front door crashed open. Marbell took one look back at the enraged mob as Lac pulled her away down the alley.

*****

36 Hours Remain

Scion heard commotion in the valley. He had a moment of panic, where he thought the commotion was from the wildfire spilling over the high cliff walls lining the eastern side of the valley and catching the houses ablaze. He shook his head. The cliffs were too high to allow the fire to come down them. The fire had to come up the valley to reach the city. Still, it would be best to see what the commotion was about. He told Pulful that he was heading up the mountain for watch duty and would return in the evening.

The Costilleja District was empty. The quiet houses sat squat in the mud, their black-eyed doorways staring vacantly into the heavy, orange air. Many houses had strung up fresh caught deer in order to drain the blood. Scion shuddered at the eerie scene of red blood soaking into the black dirt in the midst of the orange haze and moved on.

The Harebell District also lay empty but sounds of protest could be heard not much further up the valley. The houses here lay broken. Discarded goods were left scattered across the mud streets. Crying could be heard from some houses. Scion hurried onward, his feet gaining urgency as fear swelled in his chest.

The Lower Lake District fared worse than the Harebell District. The grand houses lay open to the world through shattered windows and broken doorways. Shattered glass twinkled across the cobbled streets. Yelling and the sound of looting could be heard nearby. Scion put up his hood and hoped he would not be recognized. He passed around the lake that spread its cold waters from the bottom of the cliff. The winding path that ran up the cliff to Columbine Palace was filled by a crowd slowly churning upwards. A few citizens fell. Scion gasped, then coughed as the smoke-filled air filled his lungs and coated his throat. He ran to the path and met with the back of the crowd.

He passed the few people distancing themselves from the rest of the mob. The tail end of the mass of people was more interested in watching the antics of those ahead, so they allowed the newcomer through, hoping for more of a show. The easy path soon ended, and Scion was forced to elbow and shove his way further through the crowd, reaching nearly the point where the path sloped upwards. Here people became irritated and were shouting angrily. They demanded to know what was happening. They wanted to know how the Dynast, Council, and military were helping with the situation. Scion distractedly noticed that some in the crowd were scared of the fire, while others were worried about an army from Mica. The prince understood. The orange light of the day, the red sun shining weakly above them, the smoke masking their sense of smell and taste, and no word from anyone in power, would make anyone scared.

Scion turned to his left and began pushing out to the side of the crowd. He had to get out of the mob. The crowd's fear and panic was a physical presence wrapping itself around the people, and Scion felt its cloying presence begin to eat at his own mind. He elbowed his way through the sea of people, barely paying attention to anyone but himself. Soon he splashed into the freezing snowmelt that filled the lower lake. He shivered momentarily in the frigid waters, then sighed as he let the clean water flow around his feet. He closed his eyes, trying to calm his fear-filled mind. The lake was undisturbed by the coming fire, or the rumors of war, or the shouting mob. The clear waters had no reason to be concerned. Scion wished he could be like the lake, distant, peaceful, blissfully unaware. He breathed deep and opened his eyes to the mob. It seemed almost everyone in the city was attempting to push their way up to the palace. Stopping them halfway was a group of soldiers with spears and shields. Scion spotted more soldiers lining the top of the cliff. He knew they would be armed with bows.

Scion splashed through the shallow lake and quickly arrived at the cliff face. He began clawing his way back into the crowd, moving up the steep stone path. He heard the angry shouts of the people he shoved behind him, but he did not dare stop. As Scion came to the front of the crowd, he lowered his hood and looked at the soldiers. Recognizing the grandson of their ruler they allowed Scion to pass. The yelling intensified behind Scion as he walked into the soldiers' midst.

Scion paused, then turned around. He came back to the line of soldiers and stood between the mob and the military. He raised his hands.

The first line of protestors quieted as Scion yelled, "Go back to your homes and businesses! This strange light and red sun are caused by the smoke in the air from the fire. The smoke will pass. The fire will pass. Soon we will have clear air and blue skies again. Do not worry."

"There's no fire!" Someone in the crowd shouted back. A few people yelled their agreement. "I heard this is a trick by the Micans. To frighten us. To divide us. You should be strengthening our defenses, sending out soldiers to scout for the Micans. You aren't doing anything!"

"There is no threat from Mica!" another person shouted. "They were destroyed by the fire and the fire will destroy us too. Are you blind to the ash in the air? Does your nose not work? I want to know what is being done about the fire."

Scion yelled back, "I am building a trench to stop the fire. If you are concerned about the fire then you should volunteer to help dig the trench, not be up here protesting." Scion took a step back, breathing hard. The air was thin near the top of the mountain, and the smoke did little to help with breathing.

"My nose works fine. Do your ears and brain work? Have you not heard the news of the marching Mican army? Can you not understand that this smoke is nothing but a ploy to invade us? The fire is fake!"

Scion opened his mouth to speak, but the bickering of the protestors below him drowned out anything he had to say. The people began pushing one another, then fistfights broke out. Some protestors fell from the path, and the mob as a whole fell back. The frightened mass of Bergamotians began eating itself in anxious self-loathing.

"Thank you, my lord," a soldier behind Scion said.

Scion turned to the soldier and stated, "I helped nothing. This is madness, and for what? What will this accomplish? I am going to the watchtower."

*****

34 Hours Remain

The top of the watchtower was cold even on the warmest days of the year. This was the last bastion for Bergamot, the tower above the clouds. Bergamot was the highest city, and the thin air was one of its greatest defenses. Scion huddled in his coat against the freezing breeze and peered out at the orange haze. The further mountain peaks were hidden. He could only see as far as the first trees at the tree line below. Nothing could be ascertained of the fire through the smoke, save that the fire was close, and the fire was large. Scion sent one last cursory look over the missing horizon before turning to leave. He wanted to speak to his grandfather.

The path to the palace was short but arduous. Everything was made more difficult by the proximity to heaven's dome. Scion scurried down the path of loose rocks from the summit to the upper lake and wound his way around the lake. The air was quiet, absent of the usual chirping from the pika and marmots who also claimed the mountain top as their home. Scion hoped the funny, furry animals had fled the mountain in the face of the coming wildfire. He wondered if that was what the Bergamotians should have done from the beginning.

Scion stopped outside the massive wooden doors of the palace to catch his breath and collect his thoughts. Then, he entered. The palace was a large complex designed for the comfortable living of the Dynast, his family, the councilors who wished to live in the palace and the generals of the army, as well as the retainers and families of all those significant personages. Most Bergamotians, however, never saw the tapestried halls held up by ornately carved pine columns, or the two hundred grand fireplaces carved into the faces of bears and lions and bobcats, for the first room in the palace was the throne room.

Scion entered the breezy throne room and quickly walked down the red carpet, ignoring the gold plaited columns that reached for the lofty palace ceiling. His grandfather lounged on the granite throne, a horn of wine in his hand.

"Your people are rioting and looting, and I find you here drinking wine?" Scion asked angrily.

Epath raised his eyebrows and replied, "I heard you calmed them down. You got the city folk to leave the palace path. Excellent job, Scion, those are skills that will be very useful when you take my place. However, I am still Dynast and you will not address me in such a familiar way."

Scion gritted his teeth and replied, "Fine, your majesty, I will address you as if you were as far removed from me, as you are so clearly far removed from your people. The citizens of Bergamot are scared. They do not know if there is a fire or an army coming. They feel that they are about to lose everything at any moment. You could help alleviate their pains. Go out there and tell them what is happening!"

Epath stared at his grandson in response, then took a swig of wine.

"You sack of wine!" Scion shouted, then took a few deep breaths and continued, "I am sorry, Dynast, sir. I did not presume to tell you what to do. I am just suggesting that if you were to make an announcement telling the people that there is a wild fire coming and that we are taking precautions against the fire, you could avoid riots like this in the future."

"You make a good politician once you stop being so emotional," Epath responded. "However, I am still uncertain if a fire is coming or if this is all a ploy by Mica. The scouts I have sent out have not returned. That, to me, indicates Mica is behind this and is killing the scouts. It should not be so hard to avoid a fire. Once I know for sure what we face, I will make an announcement. Now leave, Scion."

Scion bowed curtly, turned, and left.

Epath called after his retreating grandson, "Oh, and Scion, I was going to reward you for stopping the riot, but after the things you said to me, I think simply not punishing you is enough reward."

Scion grimaced and hurried outside.

*****

Day Eight: Desperate Work
18 hours Remain

The next morning found Scion working alone on his ditch. He had stayed up all night digging. The trench sank nearly to the height of a full-grown man and was twice as wide at the top. Pulful was impressed by the progress as she wandered up to the trench's edge eating her wedge of goat cheese. Scion nodded to the councilwoman and continued digging. Pulful sat down and continued eating her breakfast.

Just as Pulful finished, a new volunteer arrived and asked, "Am I too early? I'd like to help."

Scion looked up and saw Marbell standing at the trench's edge with a shovel.

"It is never too early to help someone," Pulful answered.

Marbell nodded and slid down next to Scion. She began digging furiously at the dirt. Scion watched her and noticed that her clothes were covered in dirt and her hair was disheveled. Of course, everything was dirty that day. Visible flakes of grey ash wound their way between the air currents and settled softly upon Bergamot. A warm, choking, blizzard seemed to descend upon the mountain town.

"Are all the barrels made?" Scion asked.

Marbell looked over at Scion, then her eyes widened. She bowed low and replied, "No, my lord, or well, yes."

"Stand up, stand up, I'm not the Dynast yet," said Scion. "I am glad you finished all your barrel orders. I hope you fared well yesterday during the riots."

Marbell stood up and nodded at the ground. They continued digging. Pulful joined them with the wheelbarrow and began carting off discarded earth.

Marbell spoke while prying loose a large rock, "Actually, the rioters destroyed our home. They wanted barrels, so they broke in and took what they could. My husband is fixing up the house. He made me come here because I can get food for volunteering, they took our food as well. Tomorrow we'll switch, so that he can get dinner."

They continued working in silence. Scion was angry, sad, and worried. Marbell wanted nothing more than to be so lost in the hard labor that she would not think of her ruined home.

Scion stopped working and looked up at the black, ash raining, sky. He said softly, "I have to go. We have to prepare for the worst. I must convince my grandfather to collect food to hold us over after the houses and fields are burnt. There must be an evacuation plan in place in case this moat does not work. I have to go."

Scion slowly climbed up the ditch's side and disappeared into the dark morning haze.

Marbell asked as she watched him leave, "Why does he have to do all the work? What are the council and the Dynast doing?"

Pulful responded, "We are in fast flowing rapids, rushing to the edge of a waterfall. If we all row together we will survive, but if we argue about which shore to row to, we will die. Right now we, the council, are arguing, and the Dynast has fashioned himself as nothing more than an anchor."

*****

12 Hours Remain

At noon, the order went out. The people of Bergamot were to evacuate to the mountain summit at the sounding of the Winterbane Horn, the ancient horn used to announce the ending of winter and the coming of armies. As the order was being dispersed to the people of Bergamot, groups of soldiers roamed from house to house to collect food. The soldiers kept a close tally of what each household had given as the food was carted to the watchtower for safe keeping. However, despite the soldier's assurances that the food would be given back once things returned to normal, the people of Bergamot were not happy.

Eventually, a few citizens refused to give up their food. The soldiers responded by forcing themselves into the resistant people's homes and taking what food they could find. This escalated into a few small riots across Bergamot.

Honis listened to the shouting and fighting as he dipped his feet into Lower Lake. Near him devout practitioners of Bergamot's religion followed priests in prayer for rain. Honis watched the preachers silently. One of the pious broke away from the chanters and sat down next to Honis.

"Why do you not pray with us?" the religious man asked.

"You seem to have that covered. One more voice will not sway Mount Van to collect more clouds," Honis replied.

"Then why not help dig the trench or rebuild what was broken in the riots?"

"I was helping with the ditch yesterday but rushed home when I heard about the riots. When I got home there were still some rioters left in the area. They had broken my neighbor's front door. I became angry and fought them. All I got for my trouble was a good wallop on my back and now I can barely stand straight. I can't dig, I can't help repair anything. I can only relax and wait to get better."

The pious man nodded and said, "If you had waited for your emotions to subside you would have realized that fighting the rioters would achieve nothing. Instead you should have done nothing until they had left. Then today you could have been of use. Often if you pause and wait, the correct path will open to you. If you rush ahead following nothing but your feelings, you will find yourself in the bear's den."

"Thanks," Honis growled. "I think I've realized that."

*****

9 Hours Remain

Bystan had asked again that morning if he could help dig the ditch and Servat had given the same answer, a hard "no" hidden behind flowery words. Bystan sighed as he climbed up the backside of Juniper Valley. The smoke lay heavy in the valley. Above him and to his right, a line of red lit the underside of rising smoke. The fire was near, and Bergamot, shielded from its sight, bickered in the midday's blackness. Bystan climbed faster. He wished he was a goat. The goats danced and played above Bystan as they waited for the goatherd to reach them. Bystan struggled upwards. The air was thin and choked with smoke.

That morning Bystan had loaded his few belongings on the larger goats and prepared for a long journey away from Bergamot. The decision had not been easy, however after a few sleepless nights, seeing flames and death behind his half closed eyelids, Bystan had decided to flee. He had argued with himself all morning, saying that he wanted to see the lowlands, and now was the best time to leave. He felt a little bad about taking, no, stealing, the goats, but once the fire came, Bystan knew Servat would leave the goats to die. This was better. The goats would live with him. They would survive. Bystan would survive, and that thought added strength to his steps.

The mountain peak lay barren and frigid. The far mountains were lost to black air and gloom. The nearby peaks were no more than midnight shadows under charcoal skies. The sun could not be seen. In the distance smoke rose in great pillars lit red underneath.

Bystan shuddered at the hellscape. He glanced once at the watchtower, still distant, though he too stood on the mountain crest, and then began descending the back side of the mountain.

*****

Midnight of the Eighth Day: Arrival of the End

No Time Remains

It was said in Bergamot that the best time of the year was the day the Winterbane Horn sounded. The ancient Dynast Asoh had commissioned a horn be built of such great size and such great sound that when blown the whole world would hear the trumpeting of Bergamot and the city's enemies would quake with fear. Asoh had taken her horn to battle against the Mican army. The horn was sounded once. The trumpeting echoes died, and in response came quietly, but quickly growing louder, rumbled the sounds of moving snow and tumbling stone. All that came out of that battle was the horn and the frozen bodies of both armies. No one had lived, but the mountains were peaceful for a lifetime.

In more recent years the horn was stored in the watchtower atop Mount Van's peak. The instrument heralded the coming of armies, and the end of winter, and it was the end of winter that made people love the horn. When the snows in the valley floor began melting, when the stream water could be heard chuckling under thin ice, when the singing of returning birds began to lighten the mornings, the Winterbane Horn was blown. The people of Bergamot stopped what they were doing and headed for Lower Lake. The Dynast opened the pantry and cellar and sent barrels of food and drink down the newly thawed waterfall next to the palace. The citizens below fished out the barrels, either with poles, or braving the frigid and often icy water to retrieve the party favors. Bonfires were lit and a celebration was had, for the long winter was ending, and the light of new life was returning to Bergamot.

Now the horn sounded. Its great baritone blast bounced down the dark valley in the middle of the night. This sound was not the herald of renewed growth, nor the warnings of coming armies. This sound was that of melancholic desperation. The people of Bergamot awoke, peering out of their doors, rubbing sleep from their eyes. Then, along every street, came the cries as the citizens remembered what the horn's strange blowing meant for this night.

The fire had arrived.

Atop the high cliffs that protected the valley danced the writhing mass of flames. The fire circled down around the arms of Mount Van in hunger. As the protective hug of Mount Van's ridgelines were quickly embraced by flame, the people fled higher up their valley. No thought was left for homes, or belongings as fear spread through Bergamot; a phantom fire eating the minds of the people as the real flames approached. The crush of moving people flowed through alleyways and boulevards, leaving the weak and slow behind, trampled into thick ash.

Scion ran from the watchtower, struggled through the fleeing masses, and arrived at his moat. The fire had not reached his moat yet. He shouted then choked in the ash-thick air, then shouted again.

"Break the dam!" Scion yelled.

There was no response. Scion sighed and began running along the trench towards the stream. The workers had set up a dam that, once the fire was near, could be easily opened to fill the trench with water. No one was at the trench now. Everyone was fleeing from the flames that were sure to come barreling up the valley like a moose protecting her young. As Scion approached the stream, he heard bubbling and sprinkling of water. He slowed, looking down at the trench. Water wound its cheery way along the ditch's bottom. The flow grew strong, adamant in its will to move.

"A strange night," Pulful said as she came from the stream.

Scion nodded, "It is. Were you the one who filled the ditch?"

"I figured no one else would do it when the time came, but it looks like I was wrong." Pulful nodded behind Scion.

Scion turned and saw Honis, Marbell, and Lac coming down the valley. Scion smiled as they approached and thanked them for coming. Their work was done. The moat ran deep and wide, Scion could not imagine the fire crossing such a waterwork, yet deep in his mind the worry remained.

At the head of the valley, the night was quiet. The fleeing masses from Bergamot had long since gone far up the valley and their shouts could not be heard. The animals and insects of the mountain had fled some days ago, being wiser in the ways of nature than man. For Scion and his entourage, the night was silent, warm, and stifling. White ash fell as snow upon the ground, dancing atop the spiraling waters of the stream. The obsidian trunks of trees melded into the black clouds. The air tasted of smoke; the watchers' noses filled with the ashen smell. There was peace to be found even then before the destruction. A moment to reflect in the face of coming battle.

And then it came. Softly, slowly at first. A red glow from far in the midnight forest. Then brighter and brighter the flames grew. Emboldened by new food, the conflagration rushed up the valley. The flame's dance up the mountain was accentuated with rushes of strange air currents and the snapping, exploding of branches, until the beast stood upon the edge of the moat. The fire stopped. It swayed on the far bank, the tongues of flames, tasting the air for the scent of new fuel, hungry for the timber houses of Bergamot.

Scion smiled and the onlookers whooped in admiration. The fire was stopped. The moat worked.

The flames climbed up the trunks of trees, showing the onlookers otherworldly acrobatics. A plume of sparks fled into the night as a pine tree fell. The demons of flame jumped from branch to branch, frolicking upon the highest peaks of the wooden dead. Below, the fire sprites hissed as they reached out above the water, their appendages turning to nothing but smoke.

The horde of fire continued climbing the trees, seeking fresher food. They danced and devoured, turning around one another in ever increasing frenzy, until one lone spirit was flung from the treetops. Scion watched with dread and amazement as a single tongue of flame arced over the moat, landing elegantly upon a shingle roof. One shingle burst aflame, then the next and the next. The house burned as one flame birthed a hundred.

Honis yelled in fright at the sight of the burning house. Marbell placed a shaking hand on Honis's shoulder, as much to calm herself as to calm him. Scion, Pulful, Honis, Lac, and Marbell ran. Turning their backs to the approaching monster of flame made the hair on their necks stand straight, and sent an electric shock down their spines, adding clumsy urgency to their fleeing steps. The house the flame had landed upon was lost, and soon the city would follow.

They rushed up the mountain, passing a few stragglers who had been late leaving their houses. Many people stood ready with barrels and buckets of water ready to wet the roofs of their homes as the fire approached. Scion and Pulful warned them to run as they passed, knowing that a barrelful of water, while useful against a normal house fire, would amount to nothing in the face of the beast behind them.

Near Lower Lake, Scion and his team rushed around Servat's large estate. The businessman and council leader could be heard long before he could be seen. The rich man leaned out of a high window as he ordered his servants to splash water upon his mansion's walls and empty barrels of water upon the roof.

Pulful stopped and shouted up at her colleague, "Servat, come with us! We are heading to the top of the mountain. The flames cannot feed upon the short grasses above the waterfall. We must escape above tree line"

"You go!" Servat answered back. "I will stay here with my servants. Our livelihoods are at stake here. Do you know how much money will be lost if this house catches fire? I will never be able to recover financially."

"Can you and your servants recover from death? Come with us. Grab your goats and flee from the flames without! You can recover what you lose tonight; your mansion, your wealth, for those things you can rebuild. You cannot recover yourself if you die. Come!"

Servat's servants stopped working and watched, hoping they would be released to flee to Mount Van's crown. Fear reflected in their wide eyes as they looked pleadingly to their leader. Servat scowled, opening his mouth.

Scion, seeing that Servat would refuse, yelled to the workers, "Servants of Servat, come with us. Your safety is not guaranteed if you stay here. Actually, I can almost guarantee that if you remain, you will die. Give up your employer's estate, there will be jobs when this is over. Come with us and you will be safe." Scion did not quite believe his own words. He swallowed a lump in his throat and reminded himself that they only needed to get to the tree line. They were close, but still so far from safety.

"Do not listen to them!" Servat shouted back. "If you remain, I will double your wages, and guarantee you a job for life."

The servants remained, looking from Scion to Servat, then one servant threw down his bucket and ran. The cobbles clattered and splashed with more discarded baskets, barrels, and buckets as all the servants fled. Servat shut his window in disgust.

"Come," Pulful said softly as she gently pulled on Scion's shoulder. Scion turned from Servat's mansion and continued up the mountain.

The fire ate through the Costilleja and Harebell Districts, growing in mass and ferocity as the timber houses provided kindling for the flames. Just as Scion's group reached the back of the crowd struggling up the thin winding path up the cliff wall, the conflagration reached the Lower Lake District. Scion looked up. Atop the cliff stood Columbine Palace, the massive timbers and columns stood proudly, assuring those below that there was safety in her lofty heights for those who could climb the mountain path. Somewhere in those quiet halls sat Scion's grandfather, drinking wine, unconcerned about fire, knowing the flames would not reach him.

Scion looked behind and gasped, choking on the ash filled air. The flames were close. They clawed up the mountain, great paws reaching from house to house, propelling itself forward. The people at the back of the crowd also saw the flames and began shouting in panic. They pushed and shoved those in front. Lac and Marbell disappeared into the crowd.

"Into the lake!" Scion shouted. "Swim into the lake! We will be protected there."

With that Scion splashed into the water. He paid little attention to others as he fled, his fearful mind focusing only on his own survival. Others followed. The fire rushed after them but did not dare enter the frigid mountain lake.

The lake water calmed the heir to Bergamot's throne's mind as Scion watched the land around the lake burn. He had been so close. The moat had nearly worked. If only it had been wider. If only they had more people, or more time, or had chosen a thinner spot in the valley, they may have been able to weather the wildfire. Servat's mansion lit aflame. No one escaped from the building. Scion and Pulful turned away from one tragic sight to another. They watched the people slowly crawling up the path to Columbine Palace. The smoke was thick and rising along the path with refugees. There was no escape there anymore. The path was closed by clogging ash, and soon the fire itself.

Marbell and Lac pushed their way up the path, moving from stone to stone. They coughed and spluttered their way upwards, passing those who had succumbed to the smoke and lay waiting for asphyxiation. They arrived at the thinnest section of the path, called the Lover's Roost. The path bent around a great boulder and stood open to the valley below. The boulder had split from top to bottom when it tumbled from the mountain's peak, and in the long years since, myriad wildflowers had taken shelter in the boulder's depths.

In the pushing and shoving around the boulder, Lac fell, twisting his ankle. Marbell carried Lac into the boulder's cleft, hoping to be able to help Lac up the mountain once the crowd lessened. It was quiet in the boulder. Teenagers often met here; the boulder provided seclusion from the city without having to go into the woods. For those who were lovesick, the scent and view of so many wildflowers caught in the great boulder's belly provided a reflection on nature's beauty and fragility.

The crowd moved on, thick as ever. There was no escape yet. Marbell bit her lip in worry. The Lover's Roost filled with black smoke. The flowers dipped their heads in resignation of the coming monster. Marbell and Lac waited. Flames began to slowly wind up the stunted tree growing over the boulder cleft. Marbell watched, fascinated as the thin red tongues of flame spread, like ghosts of seasons past, so small that one breath would disperse them, but soon their brethren would arrive, and all would be consumed.

The path was free. The path was nothing more than billowing, black smoke. Marbell stood, then immediately fell. Her lungs filled with smoke and ash, she coughed herself hoarse. Lac crawled over to Marbell and hugged her.

"You go. I can't get out. Can't move quick enough with this ankle," he explained.

Marbell hugged Lac harder and whispered into the crackling, spark filled air, "Bullshit. I would never leave you."

Lac smiled and whispered, "You're brighter than this fire. Please don't let the smoke blot you out."

The flames surrounded the boulder, causing shadowed silhouettes of the couple to dance along the cleft's walls. The delicate flowers of blue bells, yellow suns, and red cups bowed their heads in the heat and shed petal tears for their seasonal lives cut so short. The green lichen charred black as the surrounding stones darkened in the licking flames. Marbell and Lac hugged each other harder, trying to let the words that they could not say through their smoke choked lungs be understood through their final embrace. Both took one last shuddering breath of ash and fire and dreamed no more.

In the lake the people of Bergamot cried and shouted. They watched their proud city being eaten by flame and despaired. Their fear gone in the waters, replaced with sadness and worry. They asked what would become of them, with no homes, no belongings. They asked why the mountain had not protected them by sending rains.

Scion heard all this and was saddened. He hated to see so many people show such despair. The heir to

Bergamot climbed up a stone in the middle of the lake and addressed the people.

"People of Bergamot!" Scion declared. "Do not despair! Your homes may be destroyed. Your possessions may be gone. But we can build new homes, make new tools, replace old belongings. We have food stored to last the winter. There is wood in the forests for new houses, and if all the wood is burnt up, there is stone. Your possessions are nothing but things, replaceable things. Rejoice, for you are here in the lake alive, and you could not be replaced if you were lost to the fire. You are more precious than houses and tools and money. All you here saved the most precious things, yourselves. You claim the mountain did not provide for us in our time of need. True the mountain did not collect the clouds to make rain as he normally does but look where you are now. You stand in the lake made from snow melting off the top of Mount Van's hallowed head. This lake will save us, and this lake was provided to us by the mountain. Mount Van saved our lives. Our future is not lost."

As Scion finished his speech, clattering came from the burning city behind him. He turned and saw an elk scrambling up the city streets in panic. Branches and leaves were caught in the animal's horns. The crowd remained silent watching the elk pass by the lake, a forest spirit running away from the monster assailing the elk's home. The elk bounded up the thin path, intent upon reaching the land of short grasses above the trees where the fire would wither and die without kindling. As the elk rushed upwards the fire lightly touched the animal's crowning foliage. The leaves and branches caught in the elk's horns as began to smoke. The leaves crumpled inward, wilting, and turning black. The branch ends glowed red. The great elk reached the top of the cliff, stood upon a rock outcropping, and peered woefully at its burning home. The branches entangled on the elk's head burst fully into flame. The elk shook its head, trying to toss the small red devil from its crown. The fire stayed latched to the antlers. The animal snorted in panic and danced down the stones, bounding over the soft grasses, clattering along the lichen covered rocks, and fell, exhausted, at the base of Columbine Palace's closed timber doors.

The animal puffed and snorted, unable to catch its breath in the smoky air. Its chest rose and fell with each breath. Its hooves clattered against the entryway. Its antlers scraped the doors, leaving large marks behind and some small flames. These flames grew and climbed up the doors, looking for more favorable purchases. Columbine Palace, which was touted as being unreachable, unbreakable, soon had devils of fire rushing through the halls, destroying what they could in their frenzied glee. Scion watched from below as his grandfather's estate burnt to nothing. All was lost that night.

*****

__Epilogue__

Scion looked out from the standing stones that comprised the council chambers. Bergamot Valley wound below him. A cool breeze wafted down from the mountain peak and ruffled through the bright green grass below. The summer flowers bent their heads to the passing wind. Next to the new Dynast the waterfall surged over the cliff, and behind him lay the blackened timbers of his old home.

The fall and winter had been harsh. Many were lost in the fire and those who survived had had little time for mourning. Wounds had to be healed, temporary structures had to be built, people had to be laid to rest.

The spring provided little comfort. The citizens of Bergamot tirelessly worked to rebuild what they had lost and to plant new gardens and fields. They had watched nervously as the first grasses poked their fledgling blades through the frosty ground, hoping that the vegetation would return well enough for their livestock to feed on.

By midsummer hope and happiness had returned to the valley. The valley bloomed magnificently. The soil, flush with nutrients from the wildfire, had nourished wildflowers, grasses, and bushes. The old valley of dark green pines, white-barked aspen, and sprinkles of bright flowers was now transformed into a land of a thousand bright colors on a mat of bright green winding between the black pillars of burnt wood. It was a young land of hope with the scars of the old world just beginning to fade away.

The small town was nearly finished. All of the citizens worked together. There were no possessions yet. There was nothing to fight over or protect. There was no self-interest from anyone; there was only the dream of rebuilding and making a world better than the one that had burned. After the horror of the fire all of the people of Bergamot had set aside their differences and shared what little they could. No one quite felt at peace yet. There was still so much work that needed to be done, and everyone worked together towards that brighter future. Scion knew this idyllic period would soon end. Soon the people would rebuild their homes and businesses. They would have possessions again and things would return to the way they had been before, but for now it was wonderful to see the people work as one.

Scion smiled and looked up to the bright blue sky. Clouds had begun to slowly form over the mountain peaks in the early afternoon. He hoped the people would remember this fire and when another disaster reared its head, they would put aside their differences and work together. He hoped he would do the same. He regretted refuting Servat and Pulful's advice for the moat location. The new Dynast was determined to better listen to his councilors. Looking down at the valley, however, Scion knew that the black timbers would slowly crumble away, the charred rocks would be covered in lichen, aspen would fill the valley where pines once grew, and all the scars left by the fire would fade into nothing, as would the memory of the fire itself fade from Bergamot's mind.

But maybe, maybe, the memory of this spring and summer, a memory of working together, would remain. The memory of the laughter held by the workers after the first new roof was placed over their heads. The memory of the children yelling and dancing as the first flowers poked through the muddy, ashen ground. The memory of warm soup passed between desperate hands in the dead of winter and the tears of appreciation that came with a warm meal and companionship; the feeling of being depended on and being dependent on others. The truth that everyone was in this together, that the people of Bergamot were all that mattered, were all that would remain.

Acknowledgements

First, I would like to thank my readers. Thank you for reading my story and I hope you enjoyed the book.

Next, I would like to thank the people who helped improve the book through their early reading and suggestions. Deborah Brisbois, Kyle Jones, and Adrianne Snyder, thank you so much for taking the time to read the early draft of this novella and giving me such good advice. Your feedback was extremely helpful, and I think made this story much better. Thank you.

And lastly, I would like to thank the moderators of the redditserials subreddit on reddit.com. You set up the writing derby competition and provided me with the cover for this book. The competition was fun, and if there was no competition then this book would most likely never have been written. I hope you continue to have similar events on your subreddit in the future.

This book was written as part of the RS Publishing Derby. For the rest of the fantastic books involved in the RS writing derby go to the following website
https://www.inkfortpress.com/derby-2020

About the Author

Joseph J. R. Johnson is an engineer and author living near Denver Colorado. He is a graduate from Colorado State University with a bachelor's degree in biomedical engineering and a bachelor's degree in mechanical engineering. He enjoys skiing in the winter, playing tennis in the summer, playing boardgames with his friends, reading, and of course writing.

Other Works by Joseph J. R. Johnson

Forgiveness